GW00732800

Five-Minute Stories for Boys

hinkler

This book belongs to

_____

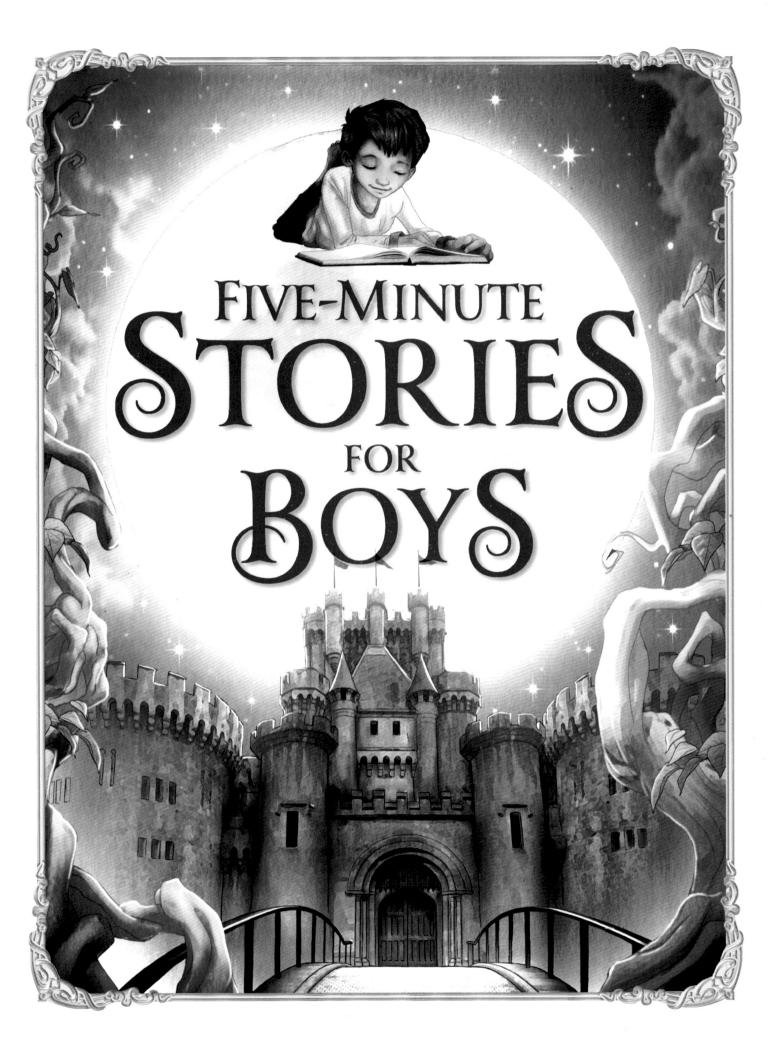

FIVE-MINUTE
STORIES
FOR
BOYS

hinkler

Published by Hinkler Books Pty Ltd
45–55 Fairchild Street
Heatherton Victoria 3202 Australia
www.hinkler.com.au

© Hinkler Books Pty Ltd 2010, 2013

Cover Illustration: Adam Relf
Illustrators: Brijbasi Art Press Ltd
Editor: Suzannah Pearce
Designers: Diana Vlad, Mandi Cole and Ruth Comey
Prepress: Graphic Print Group

ISBN: 978 1 7435 2049 9

Printed and bound in China

Contents

Introduction

For centuries, fairytales have given children their first taste of the world of books and literature. Not only are folk and fairytales rollicking good fun, whisking children away to worlds of magic and imagination, they also teach valuable lessons about how to make your way in a world that can be dark and challenging.

Our favourite fairytale characters don't always have an easy time. They meet and overcome obstacles at every turn, just as our children will – though, hopefully, not in the form of wicked witches or mischievous goblins.

Among the best-known collectors of European folklore and mythology were Jacob and Wilhelm Grimm, from Germany, and Hans Christian Andersen, from Denmark. Not only did they collect and publish fairytales that had been passed on through oral tradition for centuries, but Andersen, in particular, created original tales of his own.

A key feature of many fairytales is brevity, their authors aiming to encapsulate timeless lessons on life in short, sharp, memorable style. As the title suggests, the stories in *Five-Minute Stories for Boys* are intended to be read in around five minutes, and are great for the short attention spans of young children or busy parents. The fairytales can be enjoyed at bedtime, playtime, or whenever your family has five minutes to spare.

A love of reading and an appreciation of literature is one of the greatest gifts an adult can pass on to a child. Sharing fairytales with even the youngest children brings joy and delight and helps build and strengthen bonds of love, respect and understanding that can last a lifetime.

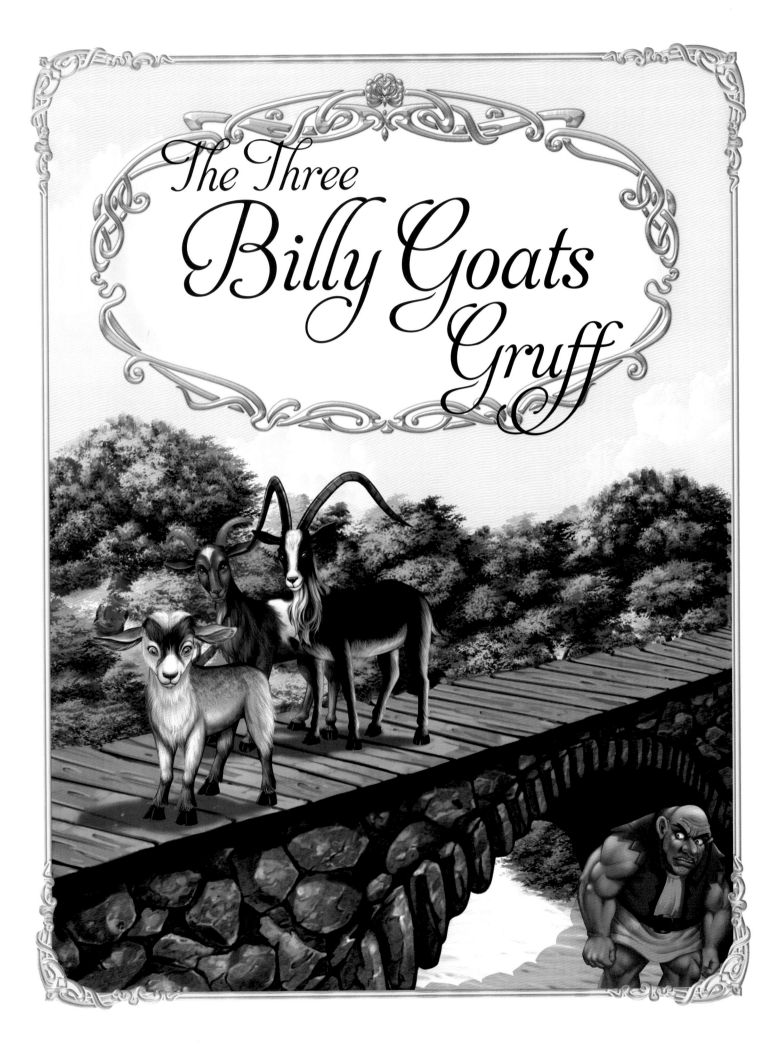

The Three Billy Goats Gruff

Once upon a time there lived on a hillside three billy goats whose name was Gruff.

Winter had passed and the lean, hungry billy goats wanted to go to the green meadow on the other side of the valley so they could eat the juicy, tasty grass and grow fat over the summer. At the bottom of the valley was a cascading stream that they had to cross. Over the stream was a bridge, but under the bridge there lived a great, ugly Troll, with eyes like big, round saucers and a nose as long as a poker.

First of all went the youngest and smallest Billy Goat Gruff.

'Trip, trip, trip, trip!' went the wooden bridge as the billy goat's hoofs danced across it.

'Who's that tripping over my bridge?' roared the Troll from underneath the bridge.

'It's me, the tiniest Billy Goat Gruff,' said the billy goat in a tiny voice. 'I am going up the hillside to eat some juicy, tasty grass so I can grow fat!'

'No you're not!' roared the Troll. 'I am coming to gobble you up!'

'Oh, please don't eat me! I'm too little, I am,' said the youngest Billy Goat Gruff. 'If you wait a little while longer, the second Billy Goat Gruff will come along. He's much bigger than me.'

'Bigger, is he?' asked the hungry Troll. 'Well, be off with you then!'

And the youngest Billy Goat Gruff tripped lightly across the bridge to the meadow.

After a little while, the second Billy Goat Gruff came along to cross the bridge. He was a medium-sized billy goat.

'Trap, trap, trap, trap!' went the wooden bridge as the second billy goat made his way across.

'Who's that trapping over my bridge?' roared the Troll from underneath the bridge.

'It's me, the second Billy Goat Gruff,' said the billy goat in a medium-sized voice. 'I am going up the hillside to eat some juicy, tasty grass so I can grow fat!'

'No you're not!' roared the Troll. 'I am coming to gobble you up!'

'Oh, please don't eat me! I'm only medium-sized, I am,' said the second Billy Goat Gruff. 'If you wait a little while longer, the third Billy Goat Gruff will come along. He's much bigger than me.'

'Bigger, is he?' asked the hungry Troll. 'Well, be off with you then!'

And the second Billy Goat Gruff trapped across the bridge to the meadow.

Then the third Billy Goat Gruff came along to cross the bridge. He was a very large billy goat.

'Tramp, tramp, tramp, tramp!' went the wooden bridge as the third billy goat stomped across it.

'Who's that tramping over my bridge?' roared the Troll from underneath the bridge.

'It's me, the third Billy Goat Gruff!' roared the billy goat in a very loud voice. 'I am going up the hillside to eat some juicy, tasty grass so I can grow fat!'

'No you're not!' roared the Troll, jumping up on to the bridge. 'I am coming to gobble you up!'

'Well, come along then!' said the third Billy Goat Gruff. He lowered his head and pointed his horns at the Troll. Then he charged!

The Troll bounced into the air and landed on the bridge. The big billy goat jumped on to the Troll and stomped him with his big hoofs. Then he kicked out his hind legs and tossed the Troll into the rapids below. The Troll floated away, black and blue, and that was the last anyone ever saw of him.

The three Billy Goats Gruff went up the hillside to the green meadow. There they ate some juicy, tasty grass until they were so fat that they could scarcely walk home again. And after that day, they went to the meadow on the opposite side of the valley whenever they wished.

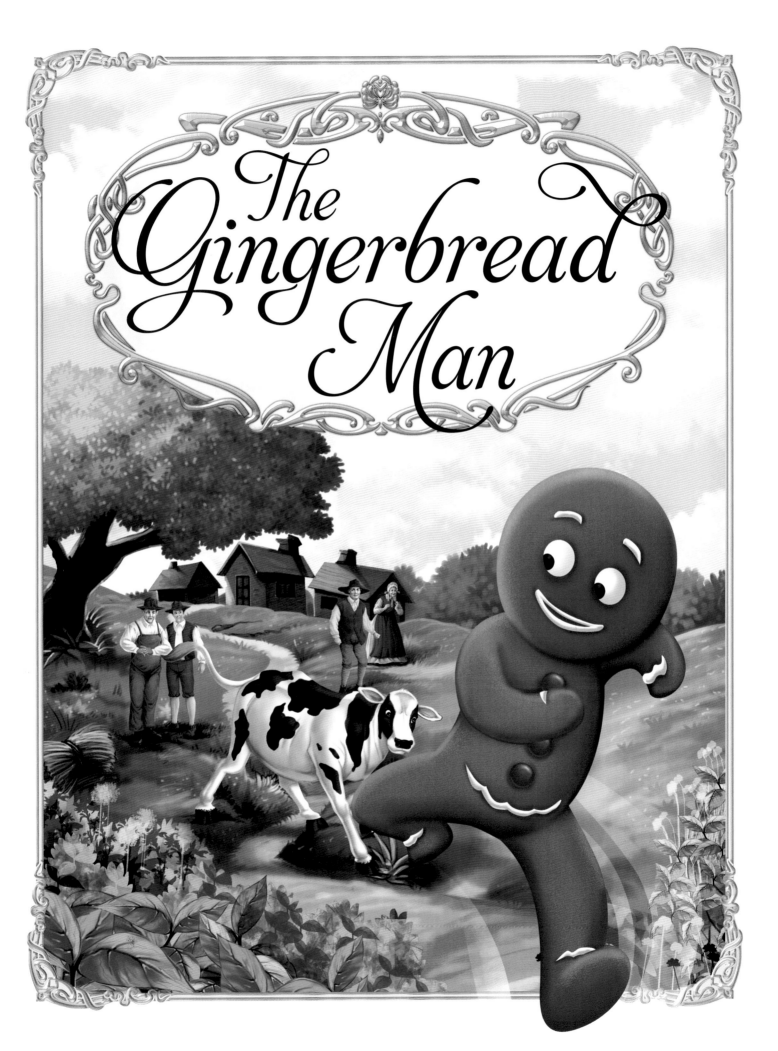

The Gingerbread Man

There was once a little old man and a little old woman who lived in a little old house on the edge of a wood. They would have been a very happy little old couple but for one thing – they had no little child and they wished for one very much.

One day, the little old woman was baking gingerbread. She cut the dough in the shapes of little boys. They had currants for eyes and cherries for buttons. The little old woman put them into the oven.

After a little while, the little old woman went to the oven to see if they were baked. As soon as she opened the oven door, one little gingerbread man jumped out and began to run away as fast as he could!

The little old woman called out to her husband. They both ran after the little Gingerbread Man, but he was so fast that they could not catch him. As he ran, he sang out:

'Run, run as fast as you can!

You can't catch me,

I'm the Gingerbread Man!'

Soon the Gingerbread Man came to a barn full of workers who were threshing wheat. He called out to them as he ran past, saying:

'I've run away from a little old woman,

A little old man,

And I can run away from you, I can!

Run, run as fast as you can!

You can't catch me,

I'm the Gingerbread Man!'

The barn full of threshers all ran after the Gingerbread Man. Although they ran fast, they could not catch him.

The little Gingerbread Man ran on until he came to a field full of mowers. He called out to them:

'I've run away from a little old woman,

A little old man,

A barn full of threshers,

And I can run away from you, I can!

Run, run as fast as you can!

You can't catch me,

I'm the Gingerbread Man!'

The mowers all ran after the Gingerbread Man, but they couldn't catch him.

The little Gingerbread Man ran on until he came to a cow. He shouted out to her:

'I've run away from a little old woman,

A little old man,

A barn full of threshers,

A field full of mowers,

And I can run away from you, I can!

Run, run as fast as you can!

You can't catch me,

I'm the Gingerbread Man!'

The cow ran after the Gingerbread Man, but she couldn't catch him.

The little Gingerbread Man ran on until he came to a pig. He cried out to the pig:

'I've run away from a little old woman,

A little old man,

A barn full of threshers,

A field full of mowers,

A cow,

And I can run away from you, I can!

Run, run as fast as you can!

You can't catch me,

I'm the Gingerbread Man!'

The pig ran after the Gingerbread Man, but he couldn't catch him.

The little Gingerbread Man ran until he came to a river. He didn't know how to swim and couldn't get across.

A sly fox was sitting by the river and saw the Gingerbread Man standing there. 'Do you want to get across the river little man?' asked the fox. 'Jump on my tail and I'll carry you across.'

'He won't be able to reach me from his tail,' thought the Gingerbread Man. 'I'll be safe there.'

The Gingerbread Man climbed on the fox's tail and the fox started swimming across the river.

A little way across, the fox's tail started drooping into the water and the Gingerbread Man was in danger of getting wet.

'You're too heavy for my tail,' said the fox. 'Get on my back.' So the Gingerbread Man climbed up on to the fox's back.

A little further across, the fox's back started to sag. 'You're too heavy for my back,' said the fox. 'Sit on my nose.'

So the Gingerbread Man climbed on to the fox's nose.

As soon as he reached the riverbank, the fox tossed his head, throwing the Gingerbread Man into the air. He snapped his mouth shut and ate the Gingerbread Man up in one mouthful. The Gingerbread Man was all gone!

'Delicious!' said the sly fox.

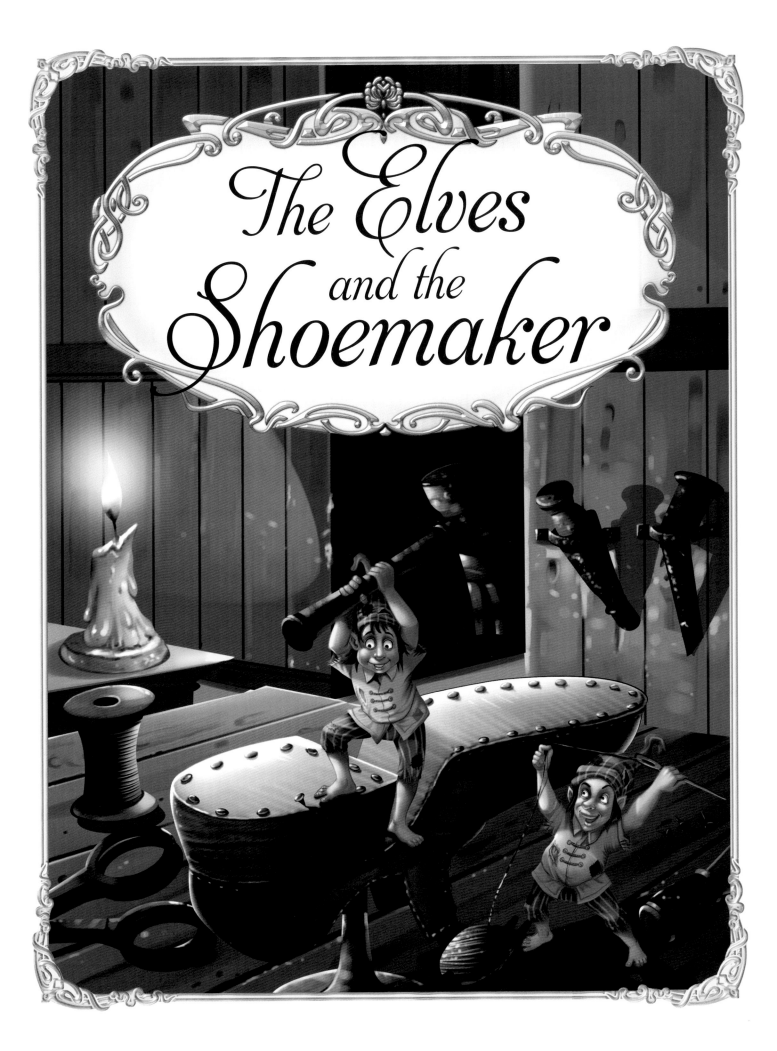

The Elves and the Shoemaker

Once there lived a Shoemaker and his wife. They worked very hard and were very honest, but they were also very poor. They could not make enough money to live on and soon everything they had in the world was gone. All they had left was just enough leather to make one pair of shoes.

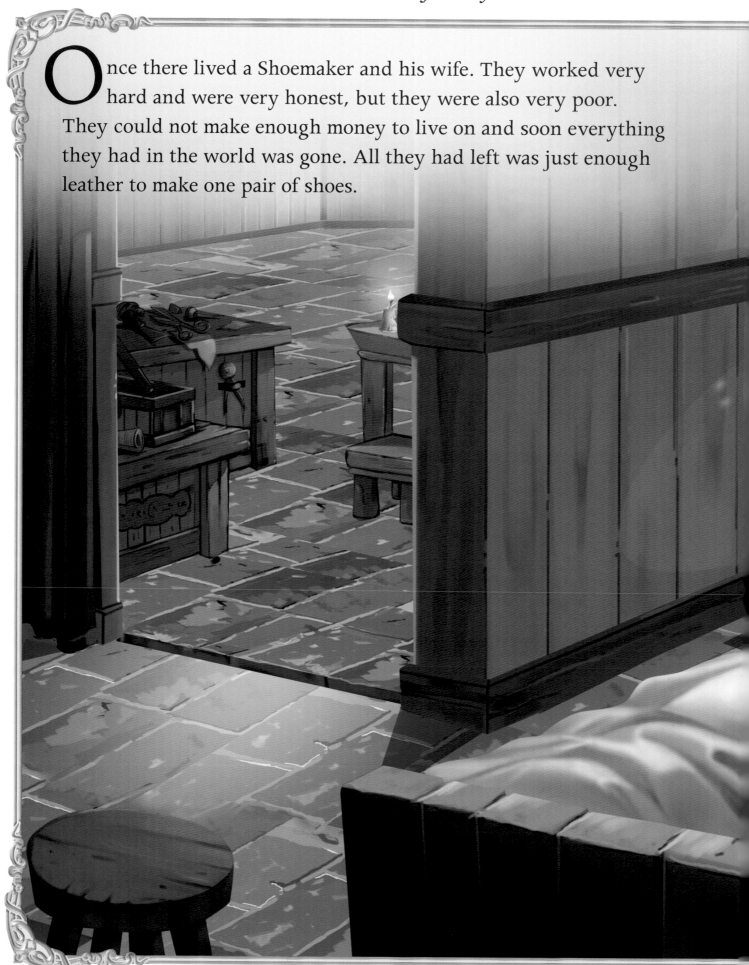

The poor Shoemaker cut out the leather and laid it out, ready to make into shoes early the next morning. 'Tomorrow, when it is sunny, I will work on them,' he told his wife. The good Shoemaker said his prayers and lay down to sleep.

The next morning, he went to start work on the shoes. However, to his wonder, he saw the shoes sitting there on the table, already finished. What an odd thing! The good man didn't know what to say or think. He looked at the workmanship on the shoes. They were so perfect, there was not a stitch wrong.

Soon a customer came in and asked to see the shoes. They suited him so well that he paid much more for them than was usual. The poor Shoemaker was able to buy enough leather to make two pairs of shoes. That evening he cut out the leather and laid it out, ready to work on the next morning.

When the Shoemaker got up the next day and went into his shop to start work, there were two finished pairs of shoes sitting there. Again, the work was that of a master. Soon some customers came in and bought the shoes, so that the shoemaker could buy enough leather to make four pairs. He cut out the leather and laid it out overnight. Sure enough, the next morning he awoke to find four pairs of shoes sitting there.

This continued on: the Shoemaker would cut out the leather in the evening and wake to find the shoes finished by daybreak. Soon the good Shoemaker's business was thriving.

One evening in winter, the Shoemaker and his wife were sitting by the fire talking together. The Shoemaker said, 'I should like to stay awake tonight and see who it is that comes and does my work for me.'

His wife thought that was an excellent idea. They lit the candle and then hid themselves behind a curtain in the corner of the room to see what would happen.

Right on the stroke of midnight, two little Elves dressed in ragged clothes with bare feet skipped in. They sat down on the Shoemaker's bench and picked up the cut-out leather. Their little fingers flew as their needles stitched back and forth and their little hammers rap-a-tap-tapped.

'Poor fellows! They must be so cold,' whispered the Shoemaker's wife, and indeed, they were shivering as they worked.

Soon, all the shoes sat ready on the bench. The two little Elves skipped and danced around the room and then they were gone.

The next morning, the Shoemaker said to his wife, 'I would so like to thank those good creatures for what they've done for us. What can we do for them?'

'Their clothes are so ragged and thin,' said the Shoemaker's wife. 'I will make them a warm woollen jacket, a shirt, a waistcoat and a pair of stockings and pantaloons each.'

The Shoemaker was very pleased with this idea. 'If you'll make them some clothes, I'll make them each a pair of shoes,' he said.

When everything was ready, instead of laying out the cut-out leather, they laid out the little outfits on the work table. Then the Shoemaker and his wife hid behind the curtain to see what the little Elves would do.

At the stroke of midnight, the two Elves skipped in. When they went to sit at the table, they saw the clothes and shoes lying there ready for them. They laughed and chuckled in delight and clapped their hands with joy.

They dressed themselves in their new outfits and danced and capered about the room. As they danced, they sang:

'Now we are so fine to see,

No longer need we cobblers be!'

Then they skipped out the door.

The good Shoemaker and his wife never saw the two little Elves again, but they lived long and happy lives and good luck was with them always.

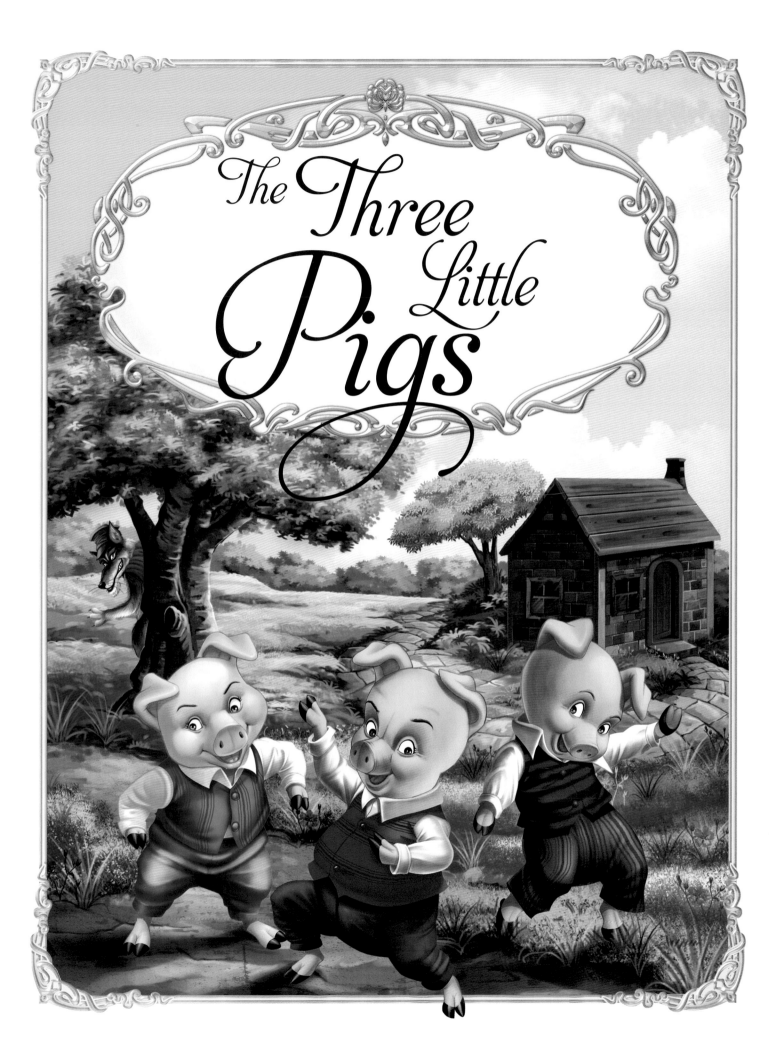

Once upon a time there lived a mother sow with her Three Little Pigs. As she did not have enough money to look after them she sent them out into the world to seek their fortunes.

As he was walking down the road, the First Little Pig met a man carrying a bundle of straw. 'Please, sir, give me that straw so I can build a house with it.'

The man gave the straw to the First Little Pig, who went and built a house with it.

As he was walking down the road, the Second Little Pig met a man carrying a bundle of sticks. 'Please, sir, give me those sticks so I can build a house with them.'

The man gave the sticks to the Second Little Pig, who went and built a house with them.

As he was walking down the road, the Third Little Pig met a man carrying a pile of bricks. 'Please, sir, give me those bricks so I can build a house with them.'

The man gave the bricks to the Third Little Pig, who went and built a house with them.

The Three Little Pigs lived happily until one day when a big bad Wolf came to the house of straw. The Wolf knocked at the door of the house made of straw and said, 'Little Pig, Little Pig, let me come in!'

The First Little Pig replied, 'No, not by the hair of my chinny chin chin!'

'Then I'll huff and I'll puff and I'll blow your house in!' cried the Wolf.

So the big bad Wolf huffed and he puffed and he blew down the house of straw. The First Little Pig ran as fast as he could to his brother's house of sticks.

Presently the big bad Wolf came to the house of sticks.
The Wolf knocked at the door of the house made of sticks and
said, 'Little Pig, Little Pig, let me come in!'

The First Little Pig and the Second Little Pig replied, 'No, not
by the hair of my chinny chin chin!'

'Then I'll huff and I'll puff and I'll blow your house in!' cried
the Wolf.

So the big bad Wolf huffed and he puffed and he huffed and
he puffed and he blew down the house of sticks. The First Little Pig
and the Second Little Pig ran as fast as they could to their brother's
house of bricks.

Presently the big bad Wolf came to the house of bricks. The Wolf knocked at the door of the house made of bricks and said, 'Little Pig, Little Pig, let me come in!'

The First Little Pig and the Second Little Pig and the Third Little Pig replied, 'No, not by the hair of my chinny chin chin!'

'Then I'll huff and I'll puff and I'll blow your house in!' cried the Wolf.

So the big bad Wolf huffed and he puffed and he huffed and he puffed and he huffed and he puffed but he could not blow down the house of bricks.

When the Wolf realised that he could not blow down the house of bricks with his huffing and puffing, he said, 'Little Pig, I know where there is a nice field of juicy, tasty turnips.'

'Where?' asked the Third Little Pig.

'In Farmer Brown's field,' replied the Wolf. 'I will call for you at six o'clock tomorrow morning and we will go together to get some for our dinner.'

The next morning the clever Third Little Pig got up at five o'clock and went by himself to get the turnips. 'Are you ready to get some turnips?' asked the Wolf, when he arrived at the Pig's house at six o'clock.

'Ready? I have already been and come back with a nice potful for my dinner!' replied the Third Little Pig.

The Wolf was very angry. He said, 'Little Pig, I know where there is a nice apple tree.'

'Where?' asked the Third Little Pig.

'In Farmer Smith's orchard,' replied the Wolf. 'I will call for you at five o'clock tomorrow morning, and we will go together to get some juicy, tasty apples.'

However, the clever Third Little Pig got up at four o'clock and went to the apple tree. As he had further to go he was still up the tree picking apples when he saw the angry Wolf coming.

'Little Pig, come down and tell me if they are nice apples,' called the wolf.

'They're very nice,' replied the Third Little Pig. 'Here, let me throw you one.' And he threw an apple so far that the Wolf had to go a long way to pick it up and the Little Pig was able to jump down and run home.

The next day the Wolf came and said to the Third Little Pig, 'Little Pig, there is a fair in town. Will you go with me at three o'clock this afternoon?'

'Very well,' said the Third Little Pig.

The Third Little Pig went off earlier to the fair and had a lovely time. He bought a butter churn and was heading home when he saw the Wolf coming. In a panic, he crawled inside the butter churn to hide and it fell over. Down the hill it rolled. When he saw the churn rolling towards him, the Wolf ran away in fright.

The Wolf went to the Third Little Pig's house and told him how he'd been frightened by a great round thing rolling down the hill towards him.

'Dear me, I hid inside the butter churn when I saw you coming and it rolled down the hill. I'm sorry I frightened you,' said the Third Little Pig.

The Wolf grew angry and swore that he would come down the chimney and eat up the First Little Pig and the Second Little Pig and the Third Little Pig. But while he was climbing on to the roof, the Third Little Pig made a blazing fire and put a big pot of water on to boil. As the Wolf was climbing down the chimney the Third Little Pig took off the lid and – splash! – the Wolf fell into the scalding water.

The Wolf howled and leapt so high that he jumped right out of the chimney. He ran off down the road as fast as he could. The Three Little Pigs lived happily ever after in the house of bricks and never saw the big bad Wolf again.

Rumpelstiltskin

Once upon a time there lived a poor miller who had a beautiful daughter. Now, it happened that the King often hunted in the woods near the miller's village. The foolish miller, trying to make himself appear more important, told the King that his daughter could spin straw into gold.

'Now, that's a talent worth having,' said the King, who was very fond of money. 'Bring her to my palace tomorrow and I'll put her to the test.'

The next day, the miller's daughter was brought before the King. He led her to a room that was full of straw, gave her a spinning wheel and said, 'Now, set to work and spin all night. If you haven't spun this straw into gold by dawn, you shall die.'

The poor girl protested in vain. The door was locked and she was left alone. She sat down and began to cry, as she had no way of turning the straw into gold. Suddenly the door opened and a strange little man stepped into the room.

'Good day to you, young lass,' the man said. 'What are you weeping for?'

'Alas!' the miller's daughter replied, 'I must spin this straw into gold and I do not know how.'

'What would you give me to do it for you?' asked the strange little man.

'My necklace,' replied the girl.

The little man took the necklace and sat down at the spinning wheel. 'Whir, whir,' went the wheel as the little man sat and spun. He whistled and sang as he worked:

'Round about, round about. Lo and behold!

Reel away, reel away, straw into gold!'

Soon the work was done and all the straw was spun into gold.

When the King came in the next morning and saw the pile of gold, he was astonished and pleased. However, his greed for gold grew stronger. He put the miller's daughter in a room with a larger pile of straw and told her that if she valued her life, she must spin it all into gold by the next morning.

Once again, the miller's daughter sat down and burst into tears.

But then, as before, the door opened and in walked the strange little man.

'What will you give me if I complete your task?' he asked the miller's daughter.

'The ring on my finger,' answered the girl.

The little man took the ring and sat down at the spinning wheel. 'Whir, whir,' went the wheel again. The little man sat and spun, whistling and singing as he worked:

'Round about, round about. Lo and behold!

Reel away, reel away, straw into gold!'

Before morning, the little man had finished and all the straw was spun into gold.

The King came in the next morning and was even more pleased with the pile of gold. However, his greed was not satisfied. He took the miller's daughter into a room with an even larger pile of straw and said, 'All this must be spun tonight. If it is, you shall become my Queen.'

As soon as the girl was alone, the little man came in and asked, 'What will you give me if I spin for you a third time?'

'I have nothing left to give,' she replied.

'Then promise you'll give me your first child when you are Queen,' said the strange little man.

'That may never come to pass,' thought the girl, 'but if I do not promise, I have no way of finishing this task.'

So she promised the little man her first-born child and he set about spinning the straw into gold. He spun away and sang:

'Round about, round about. Lo and behold!

Reel away, reel away, straw into gold!'

When the King came in the next morning, he was delighted with the pile of gold. Straight away he married the miller's daughter and she became Queen.

When her first child was born, the Queen was very happy. She had forgotten the little man and her promise.

Then one day, while she was sitting playing with the baby, the little man walked into the room and reminded her of her promise.

She sobbed and cried, begging him to free her from the promise. She offered him all the treasures in the kingdom, but the little man refused. Finally, her tears softened his heart and he said, 'I will give you three days. If you can guess my name during that time, you can keep the child.'

The Queen lay awake all night, trying to think what his name could be. She sent out messengers all over the land to find any names they could.

The next day, the little man returned and she began with all the names she could think of: Timothy, Melchior, Balthazar, Benjamin, Jeremiah and more. To all of them, he replied, 'That is not my name.'

On the second day, she sent servants out to gather all the names in the neighbourhood and had a long list of unusual and comic names: Bandylegs, Crookshanks, Hunchback and more. Still he replied, 'That is not my name.'

On the third day, as the Queen was starting to despair, one of the messengers came back. He told the Queen, 'I travelled for two days without hearing any new names, but yesterday, as I was climbing a high hill in the forest, I saw a little hut. Before the hut was a fire and around the fire a strange little man was dancing and singing:

'Today I brew, tomorrow I bake,

And the royal child I'll take.

Little does my lady dream

That Rumpelstiltskin is my name!'

The Queen jumped for joy when she heard this. When the little man came in, she asked him, 'Is your name Conrad?'

'That is not my name.'

'Is your name Lincoln?'

'That is not my name.'

'Is your name Rumpelstiltskin?'

'Some witch or devil has told you that!' the little man screamed angrily. He stamped his foot so hard that he fell through the floor up to his waist, and was forced to use both hands to pull himself out. Then the strange little man ran out of the room, leaving the child with the Queen, and was never seen or heard of again.

The Three Wishes

Once upon a time there was a poor Woodcutter and his wife who lived next to a great forest. Every day, the Woodcutter went into the forest to cut timber.

One day, the Woodcutter was working in a clearing. He had marked out a huge old oak tree, which looked like it would make many planks of wood. He went up to the tree with his axe in his hand. He swung the axe back as though he were about to fell the tree with one mighty stroke.

But the Woodcutter hadn't even made one cut when he heard a small, pitiful voice calling to him. There before him hovered a tiny Fairy, who prayed and begged him to spare the oak tree, as it was her home.

The Woodcutter was so astonished that he could not utter a word. But at last he overcame his wonder and found his tongue. 'Well,' he said, 'if it's your home then I can't cut it down. I'll do as you ask.'

'You've done more for yourself than you know,' replied the Fairy. 'To show I'm not ungrateful, I'll grant you your next three wishes.'

Then the Fairy vanished, leaving the Woodcutter wondering if he had been dreaming. He slung the axe over his shoulder and started for home.

When he got there, he sat by the fire and called to his wife. He told her what had happened, and she began to formulate all sorts of grand plans. However, realising they should act prudently, she said, 'Let's not spoil anything by being impatient. We must think things over carefully. Let's put our first wish off until tomorrow and sleep on it.'

'You are right,' said the Woodcutter. He sat back in his chair by the fire and warmed himself. 'What a fine blaze!' the Woodcutter said.

'Indeed,' replied his wife. 'I wish we had some sausages. It would be nice to enjoy them by the fire.'

Scarcely had the Woodcutter's wife finished speaking when she and her husband saw a link of sausages appear down the chimney. The Woodcutter cried out in alarm, but then realised that this was the result of the foolish wish that his wife had made. He began to scold her.

'You fool!' he cried. 'To think you might have wished for a kingdom, with gold, pearls, rubies, diamonds, fine clothes, whatever you desire! And all you wish for are sausages!'

'Alas,' replied the Woodcutter's wife. 'I've made a very bad choice. I'll do better next time.'

'Yes, you will!' exclaimed the Woodcutter. 'You couldn't have done any worse! Only a fool would have wished for sausages. A curse on all sausages! I wish a sausage was hanging from your nose!'

In a flash, the wish was answered and a sausage fastened itself on the end of her nose. The Woodcutter's wife screamed and tried to pull it off, but it was stuck. Then the Woodcutter tried to pull it off, but it was stuck fast. Then they both tried but the sausage showed no sign of moving and they were in danger of pulling her nose off.

The Woodcutter's wife cried and sobbed. 'You make a wish,' she told her husband.

'No, you make a wish,' replied the Woodcutter, who also started to cry at the state of his poor wife's nose.

They had one wish left. What were they to wish for? They might wish for something very grand, but what use was all the finery in the world if the mistress of the house had a sausage stuck to the end of her nose?

Then the Woodcutter decided he would make the best use he could of the last wish and said, 'I wish my wife was rid of the sausage from her nose.'

And the next moment the sausage fell off her nose and into a dish on the table! They were so relieved that they danced around the room for joy and then ate the sausage, which was the finest sausage anyone could wish for.

The Woodcutter and his wife didn't mind that they weren't going to ride around in a golden coach or dress in fine silk. They realised that it is much better to enjoy eating a sausage than to have one attached to your nose for the rest of your life.

The Wolf and the Seven Little Kids

There was once a goat who had Seven Little Kids. She loved them all, just as much as any mother loves her children. One day, she had to go into the woods to get some food for them all.

The Mother goat called all her children to her and told them, 'Dear children, I have to go into the woods. Now, do not open the door while I am away. You must be on guard for the Wolf. If he gets in, he will eat all of you up, and not even a hair would be left. The Wolf often tries to disguise himself, but you will recognise him at once by his rough voice and his black feet.'

'Mother dear, we will be very careful not to let the old Wolf in!' the Seven Little Kids cried. 'There is no need to worry about us.' So the Mother goat bleated and went on her way with her mind at ease.

It was not long before there was a loud knock at the door and a voice cried out, 'Open the door, my dear children! It is your Mother and I have brought something back for each of you.'

But the Little Kids knew from the rough voice that it was the Wolf at the door.

'We will not open the door!' they called out. 'You are not our Mother! Our Mother's voice is soft and gentle. Your voice is rough and hard. You are a Wolf!'

The old Wolf ran to a shop and bought himself a large piece of chalk, which he ate to make his voice soft, twisting his face up at the nasty taste. Then he went back and knocked at the door, calling out in his soft voice, 'Open the door, dear children! It is your Mother and I have brought something back for each of you.'

But the Wolf had laid one of his black paws on the window sill. The Seven Little Kids saw it and cried out, 'We will not open the door! You are not our Mother! Our Mother's feet are white. Yours are black. You are a Wolf!'

The old Wolf ran to the baker and said to him, 'Mr Baker, put some dough on my foot, for I have sprained it.'

After the baker had rubbed dough on his foot, the Wolf went to the miller and said, 'Sprinkle some white flour on my foot.'

The miller thought to himself, 'The Wolf wants to trick someone,' and refused to do it. But the Wolf said, 'If you will not do it, I will eat you up.' That frightened the miller, so he did as the Wolf asked and sprinkled white flour on his paw.

Then the Wolf went back to the goat's house and knocked on the door. He called out in his soft voice, 'Open the door, dear children! It is your Mother.'

The Seven Little Kids cried out, 'First, show us your foot!' So the Wolf put his one white foot on the window sill. When the Seven Little Kids saw that the foot was white, they thought it must be their Mother and opened the door. But no! It was the Wolf!

All the Little Kids ran to hide themselves. The first hid under the table, the second in the bed, the third in the oven, the fourth in the kitchen, the fifth in the cupboard, the sixth under the washbasin and the seventh, who was the smallest of all, in the grandfather clock. The Wolf quickly found them and gobbled them up. However, he did not find the youngest kid, who was in the clock.

After he had satisfied his appetite, the Wolf felt very sleepy. He went outside and found some green grass under a tree in the meadow. He lay down and went to sleep.

A little later, the Mother goat came back from the woods. The door was wide open, the tables and chairs were turned over, the washing bowl lay broken in pieces and the bedding had been torn off the bed. She looked for her children but none were to be seen. She called them by name, one after the other, but there was no answer until she came to the youngest. Then a soft voice cried out, 'Mother dear, I am hiding in the clock!'

The Mother goat rescued the youngest kid from the clock and learned how the Wolf had eaten her dear children. She went outside and saw the Wolf in the meadow, fast asleep on the grass. As the goat looked at the Wolf, she saw that his belly was jumping and jiggling.

'Goodness!' she thought. 'Is it possible that my poor children are still alive?'

The Mother goat sent the youngest kid inside to get a pair of scissors and a needle and thread. She quickly cut a hole in the Wolf's belly. At the first snip of the scissors, one of the kids stuck its head out of the hole. She cut a little more and one after the other, all six jumped out. They had suffered no injury whatsoever! They hugged their Mother and jumped about on the grass.

The Mother goat said, 'Quick, go and look for some big stones from the stream!'

The Seven Little Kids ran off to the stream and soon came back with seven large stones. They put the stones in the Wolf's belly and the Mother goat sewed the Wolf up so gently and quietly that he did not wake up or move.

At last the Wolf woke, feeling very thirsty. He stood up and the stones in his belly began to rattle and bump against each other. He walked slowly to the stream to drink, but when he bent over, the stones were so heavy that they tipped him over into the deep water. He sank without a trace and the Seven Little Kids danced for joy, singing, 'The Wolf is gone! The Wolf is gone!'. The Mother goat hugged her Seven Little Kids and they all lived happily, and safely, ever after.

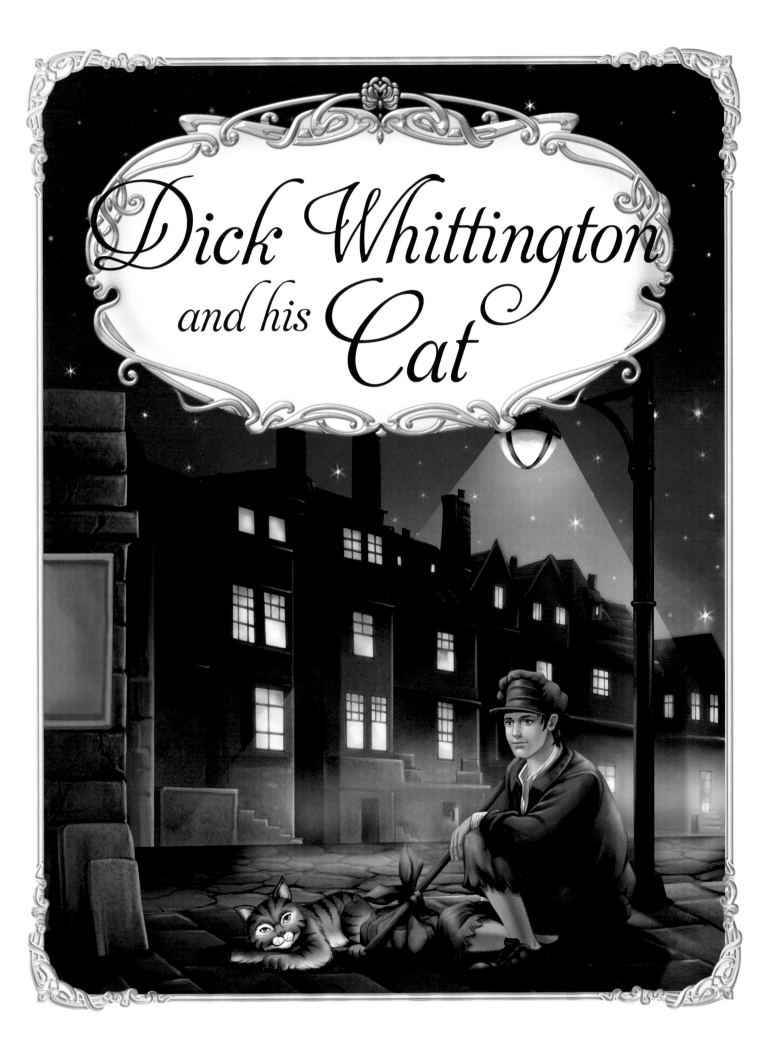

Dick Whittington
and his Cat

Many years ago, there lived a boy named Dick Whittington. His parents died when he was very young, so he was very badly off. In those days country folk thought that the people of London were fine ladies and gentlemen who were so rich that the streets were paved with gold. Dick sat and listened to all these strange tales and longed to go to London and have fine clothes and lots to eat.

One day, a wagon with eight horses stopped in the village. Dick begged the driver to take him to London. The man felt sorry for Dick when he saw how ragged and poor he was. He agreed to take Dick, and they set off immediately.

Soon Dick found himself in the wonderful city he had heard so much about. But how disappointed he was! How dirty it seemed! He wandered up and down the streets, but not one was paved with gold. Instead, there was dirt everywhere.

Dick walked until it was dark. He sat down in a corner and fell asleep. When morning came, he was very cold and hungry, and although he asked everyone he met for help, only one or two gave him a halfpenny to buy some bread. For days, he lived on the streets, trying to find some work.

One day, he lay down in the doorway of a rich merchant named Fitzwarren. He was spotted by the cook, who was an unkind, bad-tempered woman. She cried out, 'Be off, lazy rogue, or I'll throw boiling hot, dirty dishwater over you!'

At that moment, Mr Fitzwarren came home for dinner. When he saw what was happening, he asked Dick why he had been lying there. 'You're old enough to work, my boy,' he said. 'I'm afraid you're just lazy.'

'But sir, that is not so,' Dick said. He told Mr Fitzwarren about his attempts to find work and described how hungry he was. Poor Dick was so weak that when he tried to stand, he fell down again. When the kind merchant saw this, he ordered that Dick be taken inside and given a good dinner. He said that Dick could stay and work in the kitchen, helping the cook.

Dick would have been happy if it weren't for the bad-tempered cook. She did her best to make life hard for Dick. She scolded him. Nothing he did was good enough. She even beat him with the broomstick or the ladle, or whatever else she had handy.

At last Miss Alice, Mr Fitzwarren's daughter, heard how badly the cook was treating Dick. She told the cook that she would lose her job if she didn't treat him more kindly, for the family had become quite fond of Dick.

After that the cook treated Dick better, but he had another problem. He slept in an attic that was overrun with rats and mice every night. Sometimes he hardly slept a wink. Luckily, one day he earned a penny for cleaning a gentleman's shoes. He then met a girl holding a cat and bought it with the penny. Puss soon saw that he had no more trouble with rats and mice, and he slept soundly every night.

One day, Mr Fitzwarren had a ship ready to sail. It was his custom to give his servants a chance to make their fortune, so he asked them what they wanted to send out on the ship to sell. They all had something to send except Dick, who had nothing. Miss Alice said, 'I will provide something for him,' but her father told her that it must be something of his own.

'I have nothing but my cat, which I bought for a penny,' Dick said.

'Go and fetch your cat then,' said Mr Fitzwarren.

Dick fetched poor Puss. There were tears in his eyes when he gave her to the ship's captain. They laughed at his odd goods, but Miss Alice, who felt sorry for him, gave Dick some money to buy another cat.

Miss Alice's acts of kindness made the cook jealous and she treated Dick worse than ever. She made fun of him for sending his cat to sea. 'Maybe the cat will sell for enough money to buy a stick to beat you with!' she mocked.

At last Dick could bear it no longer and ran away. He walked for a while and then sat down to rest. While he was sitting, the bells of the Bow Church began to chime. As they rang, it seemed they were singing over and over:

'Turn again, Whittington, Lord Mayor of London.'

'Lord Mayor of London!' he thought. 'Why, I'd put up with almost anything for that. I'll go back and ignore the nasty old cook.' And back he went.

Meanwhile, the ship travelled far away until it came to a foreign harbour where they had never seen a ship from England before. The King invited the captain to the palace for dinner, but no sooner were they seated than a horde of rats swarmed over the dishes and started devouring the food.

Thinking of the cat, the captain said he had a creature that would take care of the rats. The King was eager to see this wonderful animal. 'Bring it to me,' he said, 'for the vermin are unbearable. If it does what you say, I will load your ship with treasure.'

When the captain returned with Puss, the floor was still covered with rats. When she saw them, Puss jumped down. In no time at all, most of the rats were dead and the rest ran off in fright. The King was delighted.

The King bought all the ship's cargo and gave the captain ten times as much for the cat as all the rest together.

Mr Fitzwarren was at his counting house when he heard a knock. It was the ship's captain with a chest of jewels. The captain told him about the cat and showed him the riches. Mr Fitzwarren told his servants to bring Dick but the servants hesitated, saying so great a treasure was too much for Dick. Good Mr Fitzwarren cried, 'Nonsense! The treasure belongs to him!'

He sent for Dick, who was black with dirt from scouring pots. At first, Dick thought they must be making fun of him. He begged them not to play tricks on a poor boy.

'We are not joking,' said the merchant. 'The captain has sold your cat and brings you more riches than I possess. Long may you enjoy them!'

Dick begged his master and Miss Alice to accept a share, but they refused. Dick was far too kind-hearted to keep it all to himself, so he gave some to the captain, the mate and the rest of Mr Fitzwarren's servants, and even to his old enemy, the cook.

Mr Fitzwarren advised him to send for some gentleman's clothes, and told him he was welcome to live in his house until he could find his own. When Dick's face was washed and he was dressed in a smart suit, he was as handsome and fine as any man who visited fair Alice Fitzwarren. She soon fell in love with him, and he with her.

A day for the wedding was arranged. They were married and afterwards treated everyone to a magnificent feast. History tells us that Mr Whittington and his lady lived in great splendour and were very happy. He became Sheriff, was made Lord Mayor of London four times, and received the honour of knighthood from the King.

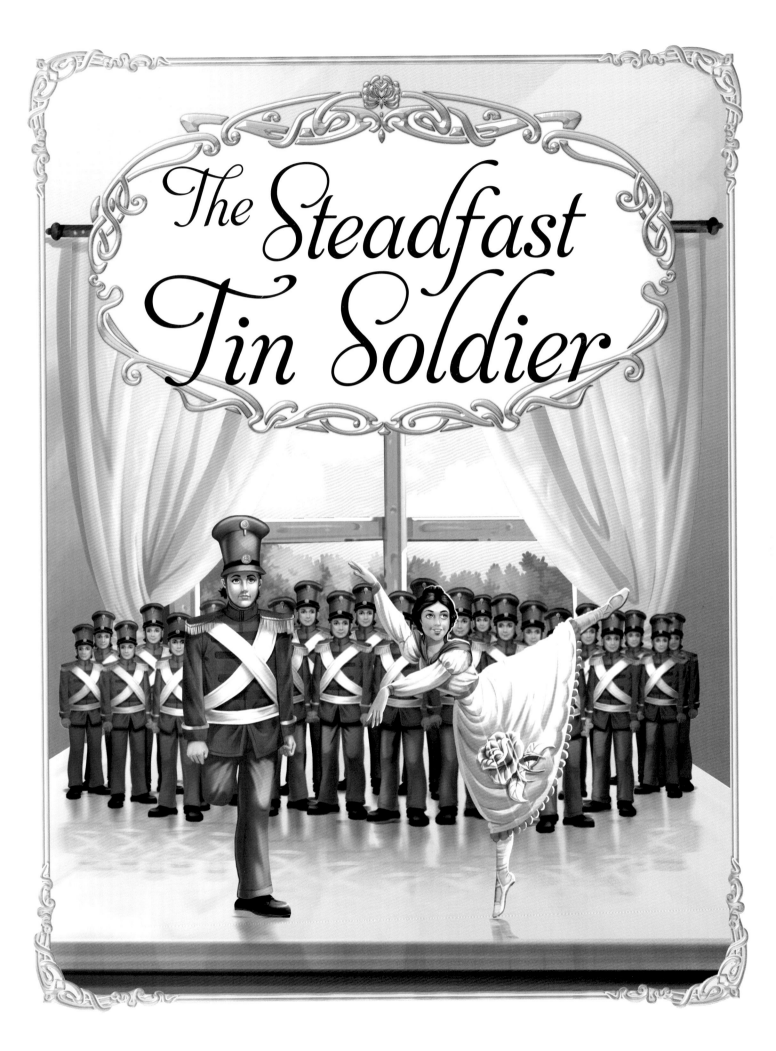

There were once twenty-five tin soldiers. They were brothers, for they had all been made out of the same piece of tin. They each stood tall and looked straight ahead and wore a splendid red and blue uniform.

The first thing in the world they ever heard were the words, 'Tin soldiers!'. The words were uttered by an excited little boy, who clapped his hands in delight when he opened the lid of the box in which the soldiers lay. They were a birthday present.

The little boy set them up on the table. They were exactly alike, apart from one who only had one leg. He had been made last and there was not quite enough melted tin to finish him, so they made him stand firmly on one leg, which made him quite remarkable.

The table on which the tin soldiers stood was covered with other playthings, but the most attractive was a pretty paper castle. Through the small windows the rooms could be seen. A number of trees stood in front of the castle, around a small mirror, which was intended to represent a lake.

This was very pretty, but the prettiest of all was a tiny little lady standing near the open door of the castle. She was also made of paper and she wore a dress of sheer gauze with a narrow blue ribbon over her shoulders like a scarf. On her dress was fastened a glittering tinsel rose, as large as her face. The little lady was a dancer. She stretched out both her arms and raised one of her legs so high that the little Tin Soldier could not see it at all, and so he thought that she, like himself, only had one leg.

'This is the wife for me,' the Tin Soldier thought, 'but she is too grand and lives in a castle. I only have a box to live in with five and twenty of us together. That is no place for her. But still, I must try and make her acquaintance.' The Tin Soldier laid himself out at full length on the table behind a snuff box so that he could peep at the delicate paper lady, who continued to stand on one leg without losing her balance.

When the evening came, the other tin soldiers were all placed in their box and the people of the house went to bed. Then the playthings began to have their own games together. They paid visits, wrestled and went to balls. The Tin Soldiers rattled in their box; they wanted to get out and join the fun but they could not open the lid. The nutcrackers played leapfrog and the pencils jumped around the table. There was so much noise that the canary woke up and began to quote poetry.

With all this activity, only the Tin Soldier and the Dancer remained in their places. She stood on tiptoe, her legs stretched out, as firmly as the soldier stood on his one leg. He never took his eyes off her, even for a moment. Then the clock struck twelve and, with a bounce, up sprang the lid of the snuff box. Instead of snuff, a little goblin jumped up, for the snuff box was a prank: it was really a jack-in-the-box.

'Tin Soldier,' said the goblin. 'Don't wish for the impossible.'

But the Tin Soldier pretended not to hear.

'Very well, wait until tomorrow then,' said the goblin.

The next morning, the children placed the Tin Soldier in the window. Now, whether it was the goblin's magic or the wind, it is not known, but the window flew open and out fell the little soldier, head over heels, from the third storey into the street. It was a terrible fall, for he came down headfirst, and his helmet and bayonet were stuck between the stones with his leg in the air.

The maid and the little boy went down to try and find him but he was nowhere to be seen.

Soon it began to rain. The drops fell faster and faster, until it was a heavy shower. When it was over, two boys came along and one of them said, 'Look, there is a tin soldier. He should have a boat to sail in.'

They made a boat out of newspaper and put the soldier in it.

The boys sent the boat down the stream of rainwater in the gutter, while they ran alongside clapping. The waves in the gutter were very high and the stream rolled along quickly. The boat rocked up and down and spun around so quickly that the soldier trembled, but his expression did not change. Suddenly the boat shot into a tunnel, and it was as dark as the Tin Soldier's box.

'Where am I going now?' thought the soldier. 'I am sure this is the goblin's fault. If only the little lady were here with me, I should not mind the darkness.'

Suddenly a water rat who lived in the drain appeared before him. 'Where is your passport?' asked the water rat. 'Show it to me at once.'

But the Tin Soldier stayed stiff and silent. The boat sailed on and the rat followed, crying out, 'Stop him!'

The stream rushed on stronger and stronger. Now the Tin Soldier could see daylight ahead and he heard a roaring sound loud enough to frighten the strongest man.

At the end of the tunnel, the drain emptied into a canal down a steep gutter, which was as dangerous for him as a waterfall was for a person. The boat rushed on and the poor Tin Soldier could only hold himself as stiffly as possible, without moving an eyelid, to show he wasn't afraid.

The boat was swept over. It whirled around three or four times, and then filled with water. Nothing could stop it from sinking. The Tin Soldier was up to his neck in water as the newspaper became soft and loose, until at last the water closed over his head. As he sank, he thought of the elegant little Dancer who he would never see again.

The boat fell apart and the soldier plunged down into the water, but immediately afterwards he was swallowed up by a large fish. Oh, how dark it was inside the fish's belly! It was darker and narrower than the tunnel, but still the Tin Soldier stood firm.

The fish swam to and fro, but eventually it became quite still. After a while, a flash of light seemed to pass through it and then daylight appeared. A voice cried out, 'Oh, I do declare! Here is the Tin Soldier!'

The fish had been caught, taken to market and sold to the cook. They placed him on a table. How strange it was to be in the same room with the same children, the same playthings, the same table and the pretty castle with the pretty Dancer at the door! She was still balancing on one leg, as unrelenting as himself.

It moved the Tin Soldier so much to see her that he almost wept, but he held back. He looked at her and they both remained silent.

Suddenly one of the boys picked up the Tin Soldier and threw him into the stove for no reason. The flames lit up the little Tin Soldier and the heat was terrible, but whether it was from the fire or from love, he could not say. He looked at the little lady and she looked at him. He started to melt away, but he remained steadfast, with his arms at his side.

Suddenly a draught of air picked up the little Dancer. She fluttered like a fairy right into the stove by the Tin Soldier's side. She instantly burst into flames and was gone. The Tin Soldier melted down into a lump and the next morning, as the maid was cleaning out the stove, she found him melted into the shape of a little tin heart. Nothing remained of the little Dancer but the tinsel rose, which was burnt as black as a cinder.